BOBBY BEAR GOES TO THE BEACH

written by KAY D. OANA

illustrations by MARILUE

published by

ODDO PUBLISHING

Fayetteville, Georgia

Symbol for exciting book ideas

Dedicated to

ROCHELLE, KEVIN, and MINDY

Library of Congress Catalog Number 80-82951.
ISBN 0-87783-153-X.
Printed in the United States of America.

Bobby woke up.
The sun was bright.
He said to Bunny,
“This day’s a delight.

"Bluebird! Bunny!
Don't sleep all day.
Let's go to the beach
To run and play.

"Let's ask my
Cousin Boo.
She likes to play
At the beach, too."

The bears, bird, and bunny,
At the edge of the bay,
Sat on the beach
To watch and play.

"The sun is yellow,
That boat is red.
See all the colors!"
Bobby Bear said.

By the water's edge
Little waves lapped.
Against the sand
Little waves slapped.

Sandpipers running,
Running on the beach,
Running toward the shore,
The bay's shore to reach.

Sailboats were sailing
In the cool breeze,
Out on the bay
Away from the trees.

They watched the boats
Sailing by,
Not one little cloud
In the bright, blue sky.

Grandpa Bear
And Cousin Boo
Both played ball
In the sea so blue.

"Let's build a castle
Tall and grand.
A pail of water
Makes sticky sand!"

Boo said, "Look!
Those birds are funny!"
"Those are sea gulls,"
Said the bunny.

"From air to sea,
From sea to air,
They are fishing,"
Said Bobby Bear.

Then Bobby said,
"See what I found.
A pretty seashell,
Smooth and round."

“I found one, too.
Mine is funny!
Let’s dig for more,”
said the bunny.

"What is this
In the pail?
I think," said Boo,
"It's a little snail."

Bobby saw a hole.
"What do you see?
A ghost crab
Is looking for me!"

Grandpa said,
"There are many shells,
Clams and mussels,
Shaped like bells."

"What are those bears
Doing over there?
Do you know?"
Asked Bobby Bear.

"They trap fish.
They use a net.
Gee," said Bunny,
"They must get wet!

"The bears put nets
Down in the sea.
They catch fish.
Let's look and see.

"The fish they catch
Are fresh and sweet.
The fish they catch
Are good to eat.

"Look, Bobby,
Look and see.
They caught a trout
As big as me!"

“They catch lobster,
That’s what they do,
Catfish and flounder
And other fish, too.”

Out in the water
They saw a buoy
Bobbing up and down
Like a small toy.

"The buoy," said Bobby,
"Has a light
To warn the ships
Through the night."

A foghorn blew,
"H-O-O, hoo, H-O-O, hoo,
We wouldn't want
To crash into you!"

A wave came closer
With a small roar.
It washed the castle
Right off the shore!

"It's getting late.
I'd better get Boo.
You get Bluebird
And Grandpa, too!"

“The tide is coming!
We’d better not roam,”
Said Bobby Bear,
“Let’s head for home.”

They hurried home,
Skipped all the way.
Bobby Bear said,
"What a fun day!"

about the author

Kay D. Oana is an Akron schools guidance counselor. She received her Bachelors and Masters Degrees from the University of Akron where she has been on the staff as a special instructor.

Her first stories were published when she was 12 years old. Since then, she has had many articles published in professional and business magazines, educational and technical periodicals, and local media. She has assisted in writing courses of study, school material and exercises, and acted as a consultant for textbook companies. Recently, Kay authored OPPORTUNITIES IN COUNSELING AND GUIDANCE in the field of vocational guidance.

Kay likes children of all ages, sizes, shapes, and forms. Her source of inspiration is the ". . . young people I counsel, enjoy, and love."

Kay has written seven books for Oddo Publishing, including: ROBBIE AND THE RAGGEDY SCARECROW, SHASTA AND THE SHE-BANG MACHINE, THE LITTLE DOG WHO WOULDN'T BE, BOBBY BEAR AND THE BLIZZARD, BOBBY BEAR GOES TO THE BEACH, TIMMY TIGER AND THE BUTTERFLY NET, and TIMMY TIGER AND THE MASKED BANDIT.

about the illustrator

Marilue Johnson was born in Grand Forks, North Dakota. She studied at Walker Art School in Minneapolis, Minnesota, and was awarded a scholarship in 1950. Her broad spectrum of experience includes: teaching art; working for leading agencies in the Midwest; murals; commissioned paintings and sculptures; and, art director for Univac Educational Division. Her biography appears in Outstanding Women of America, North Dakota Artists, Contemporary Authors, and International Authors and Writers Who's Who. She is also a member of the International Platform Society, lecturing to schools and various organizations.

Some of the books Marilue has illustrated are: BOBBY BEAR AND THE BEES, BOBBY BEAR AND THE BLIZZARD, BOBBY BEAR FINDS MAPLE SUGAR, BOBBY BEAR GOES TO THE BEACH, BOBBY BEAR GOES FISHING, BOBBY BEAR IN THE SPRING, BOBBY BEAR'S ROCKET RIDE, BOBBY BEAR'S HALLOWEEN, PRAIRIE DOG TOWN, WHEN JESUS WAS A LAD, THE ORDERLY CRICKET, MONGOOSE MAGOO, and SECRETS OF THE ABC'S. Marilue is both the author and illustrator of BOBBY BEAR'S NEW HOME, BOBBY BEAR'S RED RAFT, BOBBY BEAR'S CHRISTMAS, BOBBY BEAR'S THANKSGIVING, and BOBBY BEAR MEETS COUSIN BOO.

Marilue's husband, Harold, is a noted designer in his own right. They have two lovely daughters, Laurel and Delph, and reside in Minnesota in a home designed by Harold.